Walt Disney's

Rip Van Goofy

 Book Two

DISNEY PRESS

New York

Copyright © 2005, 2011 Disney Enterprises, Inc.

Adapted from *Rip Van Goofy,*
witten by Laura Driscoll

All rights reserved. Published by Disney Press, an imprint of Disney Book Group.
No part of this book may be reproduced or transmitted in any form or by any means,
electronic or mechanical, including photocopying, recording, or by any information
storage and retrieval system, without written permission from the publisher.
For information address Disney Press, 114 Fifth Avenue, New York, NY 10011-5690.

Printed in China

First Edition
1 3 5 7 9 10 8 6 4 2

ISBN 978-1-4231-4900-2
T425-2382-5-11123

For more Disney Press fun,
visit www.disneybooks.com

ONCE UPON A TIME, in a sleepy little village, there lived a friendly young fellow named Rip Van Goofy. On most days, you could find him sitting outside the village inn, chatting with his friends Mickey Van Bummel, the schoolmaster, and Horace Vedder, the owner of the inn.

One sunny day, Rip Van Goofy went to the inn. He was ready for some good fishing and a long nap. He wanted to know if Mickey or Horace would go with him to his favorite fishing hole.

"No, I'd best stay here and keep an eye on the inn," said Horace.

"And I don't have a pole," said Mickey. "But you have a good time, Rip."

And so it was that Rip Van Goofy set out alone on that sunny day.

Rip waved to his friends and began to walk along a dusty country road. On his way out of town, he stopped to talk to his friend Clarabelle. After a few minutes, he set off again. A couple miles later, he saw a big, crooked tree.

"Here's my turn," he said and walked through the woods. In no time at all, he came to his favorite fishing spot.

Rip Van Goofy sat down on the soft grass and dropped his fishing line into the water. "This is the life," he said as he leaned against a moss-covered rock.

Rip kept one eye on his line, watching for any sign of a nibble, while he closed the other eye. He spent most of the afternoon half awake.

As night began to fall, Rip Van Goofy's other eye closed, and he fell into a deep, deep sleep.

Bright sunshine awakened Rip. He sat up and rubbed his eyes. Last he knew, it had been early evening. Now it was morning.

Well, golly, he thought, could I really have slept here all night long?

Rip reached for his fishing pole. The metal reel, which had been quite shiny and new when he'd fallen asleep, was now completely rusted. And his wooden rod looked much more worn than he remembered.

"Now, that's strange," said Rip, and he began to rub his chin.

But even stranger was realizing that he had a long, gray beard. Rip wondered if he was still dreaming. How could a fellow grow a foot-long beard overnight?

Confused, he rose to his feet, picked up his rusty fishing rod, and began to walk back to the village.

As Rip Van Goofy reached the edge of town,
he caught a glimpse of himself in a window.

Rip gasped. Who was that old man staring
back at him? He barely recognized himself!

Eventually, Rip found himself walking through the center of the village. But instead of the sleepy little place he remembered, he found a bustling town!

Stranger still, Rip Van Goofy didn't recognize anyone. No one seemed to know him, either. Everyone seemed as confused as he was!

Rip Van Goofy walked to the village inn, where he used to chat with his friends. Surely that would still be the same. But the inn was gone. In its place stood a restaurant called Vedder's Vittles.

An old man sat in a rocking chair on the porch.

"Excuse me," Rip said to the man. "Do you know a Horace Vedder?"

The fellow in the chair peered over his glasses at Rip.

"Horace Vedder used to own this place," he replied. "But he sold it to me before he moved away. That was thirty years ago."

Rip's head was spinning. Nothing made sense! How could Horace Vedder have left town thirty years ago when Rip had just seen him the day before? Rip was at his wit's end.

"Well, golly, does anybody here know Rip Van Goofy?" he cried out in frustration.

"Rip Van Goofy?" asked the old fellow, rising slowly to his feet. "Is that really you?"

Rip heard something familiar in the old man's voice. He looked closely at him. Then, suddenly, he realized it was . . .

"Mickey Van Bummel?" Rip said, puzzled at his friend's changed appearance. "But you look so old!"

Rip Van Goofy didn't know what to think. His friend looked so different, surely he must be telling the truth about how much time had passed. But Rip could not remember any of it. What had happened to him?

"The last time I saw you was that day you went fishing forty years ago," Mickey Van Bummel recalled. "When you didn't come back, we went looking for you. But we didn't know where your special fishing spot was. You had never taken any of us there! Where have you been all this time?"

Suddenly, as Rip thought about the day's events, all the pieces of the puzzle came together: the rusted fishing reel, the long beard, the changes to the village . . . He had been asleep for forty years!

Rip told Mickey Van Bummel his remarkable story. Before long, the tale had become a legend for miles around. Since Rip Van Goofy was still just as easygoing as he was on the day he left, he soon became popular with everyone in town all over again.

He and Mickey Van Bummel loved to pass the time sitting in front of the restaurant, chatting about the old days, and talking for hours.

Rip also still enjoyed fishing and napping . . .
and napping while fishing.

But now, before he dozed off, he always made
sure there was someone around to wake him up—
just in case.